Green Eggs and Ham
and other stories

By Dr. Seuss

CONTENTS

CARNIVAL

Green Eggs and Ham and other stories
™ & © Dr. Seuss Enterprises, L.P. 2001
All rights reserved

This omnibus edition first published 2001 by Carnival,
an imprint of HarperCollins*Publishers* Ltd
77-85 Fulham Palace Road, London W6 8JB

The HarperCollins website address is:
www.**fire**and**water**.com

2 4 6 8 10 9 7 5 3 1

ISBN 0-00-763485-4
ISBN 0-00-763700-4

Printed and bound in Slovenia

Green Eggs and Ham

By Dr. Seuss

That Sam-I-am!

That Sam-I-am!

I do not like

that Sam-I-am!

Do you like

green eggs and ham?

I do not like them,
Sam-I-am.
I do not like
green eggs and ham.

Would you like them
here or there?

I would not like them
here or there.
I would not like them
anywhere.
I do not like
green eggs and ham.
I do not like them,
Sam-I-am.

Would you like them
in a house?
Would you like them
with a mouse?

I do not like them
in a house.
I do not like them
with a mouse.
I do not like them
here or there.
I do not like them
anywhere.
I do not like green eggs and ham.
I do not like them, Sam-I-am.

Would you eat them
in a box?
Would you eat them
with a fox?

Not in a box.

Not with a fox.

Not in a house.

Not with a mouse.

I would not eat them here or there.

I would not eat them anywhere.

I would not eat green eggs and ham.

I do not like them, Sam-I-am.

Would you? Could you?

In a car?

Eat them! Eat them!

Here they are.

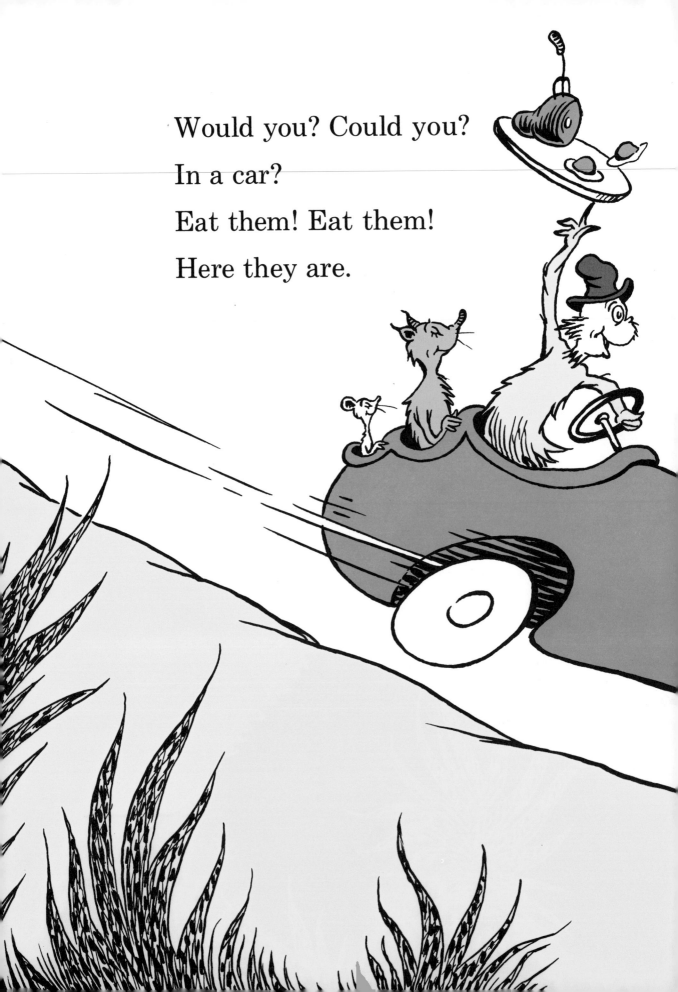

I would not,
could not,
in a car.

You may like them.
You will see.
You may like them
in a tree!

I would not, could not in a tree.

Not in a car! You let me be.

I do not like them in a box.

I do not like them with a fox.

I do not like them in a house.

I do not like them with a mouse.

I do not like them here or there.

I do not like them anywhere.

I do not like green eggs and ham.

I do not like them, Sam-I-am.

A train! A train!
A train! A train!
Could you, would you,
on a train?

Not on a train! Not in a tree!
Not in a car! Sam! Let me be!

I would not, could not, in a box.
I could not, would not, with a fox.
I will not eat them with a mouse.
I will not eat them in a house.
I will not eat them here or there.
I will not eat them anywhere.
I do not eat green eggs and ham.
I do not like them, Sam-I-am.

Say!

In the dark?

Here in the dark!

Would you, could you, in the dark?

I would not, could not,
in the dark.

Would you, could you,
in the rain?

I would not, could not, in the rain.

Not in the dark. Not on a train.

Not in a car. Not in a tree.

I do not like them, Sam, you see.

Not in a house. Not in a box.

Not with a mouse. Not with a fox.

I will not eat them here or there.

I do not like them anywhere!

You do not like
green eggs and ham?

I do not
like them,
Sam-I-am.

Could you, would you,

with a goat?

I would not,
could not,
with a goat!

Would you, could you,

on a boat?

I could not, would not, on a boat.

I will not, will not, with a goat.

I will not eat them in the rain.

I will not eat them on a train.

Not in the dark! Not in a tree!

Not in a car! You let me be!

I do not like them in a box.

I do not like them with a fox.

I will not eat them in a house.

I do not like them with a mouse.

I do not like them here or there.

I do not like them ANYWHERE!

I do not like
green eggs
and ham!

I do not like them,

Sam-I-am.

You do not like them.

So you say.

Try them! Try them!

And you may.

Try them and you may, I say.

Sam!

If you will let me be,

I will try them.

You will see.

Sam!

I like green eggs and ham!

I do! I like them, Sam-I-am!

And I would eat them in a boat.

And I would eat them with a goat . . .

And I will eat them in the rain.

And in the dark. And on a train.

And in a car. And in a tree.

They are so good, so good, you see!

So I will eat them in a box.

And I will eat them with a fox.

And I will eat them in a house.

And I will eat them with a mouse.

And I will eat them here and there.

I will eat them ANYWHERE!

I do so like
green eggs and ham!
Thank you!
Thank you,
Sam-I-am!

Did I ever tell you that Mrs. McCave
Had twenty-three sons and she named them all Dave?

Well, she did. And that wasn't a smart thing to do.
You see, when she wants one and calls out, "Yoo-Hoo!
Come into the house, Dave!" she doesn't get *one*.
All twenty-three Daves of hers come on the run!

This makes things quite difficult at the McCaves'
As you can imagine, with so many Daves.
And often she wishes that, when they were born,
She had named one of them Bodkin Van Horn
And one of them Hoos-Foos. And one of them Snimm.
And one of them Hot-Shot. And one Sunny Jim.
And one of them Shadrack. And one of them Blinkey.
And one of them Stuffy. And one of them Stinkey.
Another one Putt-Putt. Another one Moon Face.
Another one Marvin O'Gravel Balloon Face.
And one of them Ziggy. And one Soggy Muff.
One Buffalo Bill. And one Biffalo Buff.
And one of them Sneepy. And one Weepy Weed.
And one Paris Garters. And one Harris Tweed.
And one of them Sir Michael Carmichael Zutt
And one of them Oliver Boliver Butt
And one of them Zanzibar Buck-Buck McFate...
But she didn't do it. And now it's too late.

The rabbit felt mighty important that day
On top of the hill in the sun where he lay.
He felt SO important up there on that hill
That he started to brag, as animals will
And he boasted out loud, as he threw out his chest,
"Of all of the beasts in the world, I'm the best!
On land, and on sea . . . even up in the sky
No animal lives who is better than I!"

"What's *that?*" growled a voice that was terribly gruff.
"Now why do you say such ridiculous stuff?"
The rabbit looked down and he saw a big bear.
"*I'm* best of the beasts," said the bear. "And so there!"

"You're not!" snapped the rabbit. "I'm better than you!"
"Pooh!" the bear snorted. "Again I say Pooh!
You talk mighty big, Mr. Rabbit. That's true.
But how can you prove it? **Just what can you DO?**"

"Hmmmm..." thought the rabbit,
"Now what CAN I do...?"
He thought and he thought. Then he finally said,
"Mr. Bear, do you see these two ears on my head?
My ears are so keen and so sharp and so fine
No ears in the world can hear further than mine!"

"Humpf!" the bear grunted. He looked at each ear.
"You *say* they are good," said the bear with a sneer,
"But how do *I* know just how far they can hear?"

"I'll prove," said the rabbit, "my ears are the best.
You sit there and watch me. I'll prove it by test."
Then he stiffened his ears till they both stood up high
And pointed straight up at the blue of the sky.
He stretched his ears open as wide as he could.
"*Shhh!* I am listening!" he said as he stood.
He listened so hard that he started to sweat
And the fur on his ears and his forehead got wet.

For seven long minutes he stood. Then he stirred
And he said to the bear, "Do you know what I heard?
Do you see that far mountain . . . ? It's ninety miles off.
There's a fly on that mountain. I just heard him cough!
Now the cough of a fly, sir, is quite hard to hear
When he's ninety miles off. But I heard it quite clear.
So you see," bragged the rabbit, "it's perfectly true
That my ears are the best, so I'm better than you!"

The bear, for a moment, just sulked as he sat
For he knew that *his* ears couldn't hear things like *that*.
"This rabbit," he thought, "made a fool out of me.
Now *I've* got to prove that I'm better than he."
So he said to the rabbit, "You hear pretty well.
You can hear ninety miles. *But how far can you smell?*
I'm the greatest of smellers," he bragged. "See my nose?
This nose on my face is the finest that grows.
My nose can smell *any*thing, both far and near.
With my nose I can smell twice as far as you hear!"

"You can't!" snapped the rabbit.

"I can!" growled the bear

And he stuck his big nose 'way up high in the air.

He wiggled that nose and he sniffed and he snuffed.

He waggled that nose and he whiffed and he whuffed.

For more than ten minutes he snaff and he snuff.

Then he said to the rabbit, "I've smelled far enough."

"All right," said the rabbit. "Come on now and tell
Exactly how far is the smell that you smell?"

"Oh, I'm smelling a *very* far smell," said the bear.
"Away past that fly on that mountain out there.
I'm smelling past many great mountains beyond
Six hundred miles more to the edge of a pond."

"And 'way, 'way out there, by the pond you can't see,
Is a very small farm. On the farm is a tree.
On the tree is a branch. On the branch is a nest,
A very small nest where two tiny eggs rest.
Two hummingbird eggs! Only half an inch long!
But my nose," said the bear, "is so wonderfully strong,
My nose is so good that I smelled without fail
That the egg on the left is a little bit stale!
And *that* is a thing that no rabbit can do.
So you see," the bear boasted, "I'm better than you!
My smeller's so keen that it just can't be beat..."

"What's that?" called a voice
From 'way down by his feet.
The bear and the rabbit looked down at the sound,
And they saw an old worm crawling out of the ground.

"Now, boys," said the worm, "you've been bragging a lot.
You both think you're great. But *I* think you are not.
You're not half as good as a fellow like me.
You hear and you smell. *But how far can you SEE?*
Now, *I'm* here to prove to you big boasting guys
That your nose and your ears aren't as good as my eyes!"

And the little old worm cocked his head to one side
And he opened his eyes and he opened them wide.
And they looked far away with a strange sort of stare
As if they were burning two holes in the air.
The eyes of that worm almost popped from his head.
He stared half an hour till his eyelids got red.
"That's enough!" growled the bear.
"Tell the rabbit and me
How far did you look and just what did you see?"

"Well, boys," the worm answered, "that look that I took
Was a look that looked further than *you'll* ever look!
I looked 'cross the ocean, 'way out to Japan.
For I can see further than anyone can.
There's no one on earth who has eyesight that's finer.
I looked past Japan. Then I looked across China.
I looked across Egypt; then took a quick glance
Across the two countries of Holland and France.
Then I looked across England and, also, Brazil.
But I didn't stop there. I looked much farther still.

"And I kept right on looking and looking until
I'd looked round the world and right back to this hill!
And I saw on this hill, since my eyesight's so keen,
The two biggest fools that have ever been seen!
And the fools that I saw were none other than you,
Who seem to have nothing else better to do
Than sit here and argue who's better than who!"

Then the little old worm gave his head a small jerk
And he dived in his hole and went back to his work.

WHAT WAS I SCARED OF?

W_{ell}...

I was walking in the night
And I saw nothing scary.
For I have never been afraid
Of anything. Not very.

Then I was deep within the woods
When, suddenly, I spied them.
I saw a pair of pale green pants
With nobody inside them!

I wasn't scared. But, yet, I stopped.
What *could* those pants be there for?
What *could* a pair of pants at night
Be standing in the air for?

And then they moved! Those empty pants!
They kind of started jumping.
And then my heart, I must admit,
It kind of started thumping.

So I got out. I got out fast
As fast as I could go, sir.
I wasn't scared. But pants like that
I did not care for. No, sir.

After that, a week went by.
Then one dark night in Grin-itch
(I had to do an errand there
And fetch some Grin-itch spinach)...
Well, I had fetched the spinach.
I was starting back through town
When those pants raced round a corner
And they almost knocked me down!

I lost my Grin-itch spinach
But I didn't even care.
I ran for home! Believe me,
I had really had a scare!

Now, bicycles were never made
For pale green pants to ride 'em,
Especially spooky pale green pants
With nobody inside 'em!

And the NEXT night, I was fishing
For Doubt-trout on Roover River
When those pants came rowing toward me!
Well, I began to shiver.

And by now I was SO frightened
That, I'll tell you, but I hate to...
I screamed and rowed away and lost
My hook and line and bait, too!

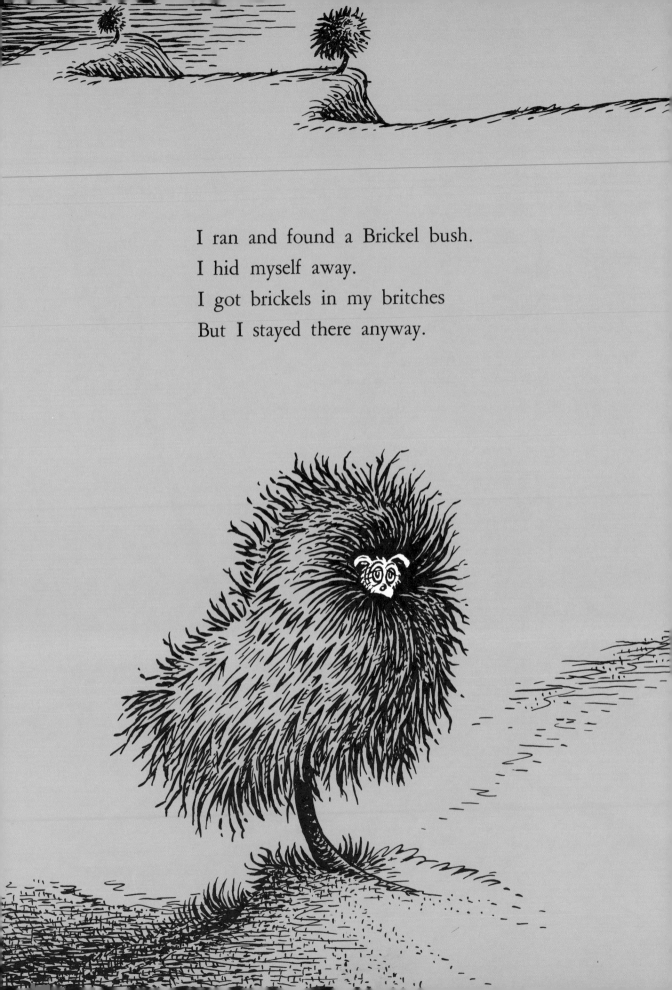

I ran and found a Brickel bush.
I hid myself away.
I got brickels in my britches
But I stayed there anyway.

I stayed all night. The next night, too.
I'd be there still, no doubt,
But I had to do an errand
So, the *next* night, I went out.

I had to do an errand,
Had to pick a peck of Snide
In a dark and gloomy Snide-field
That was almost nine miles wide.

I said, "I do not fear those pants
With nobody inside them."
I said, and said, and said those words.
I said them. But I lied them.

Then I reached inside a Snide bush
And the next thing that I knew,
I felt my hand touch someone!
And I'll bet that you know who.

And there I was! Caught in the Snide!
And in that dreadful place
Those spooky, empty pants and I
Were standing face to face!

I yelled for help. I screamed. I shrieked.
I howled. I yowled. I cried,
"Oh, save me from these pale green pants
With nobody inside!"

But then a strange thing happened.
Why, those pants began to cry!
Those pants began to tremble.
They were just as scared as I!

I never heard such whimpering
And I began to see
That I was just as strange to them
As they were strange to me!

I put my arm around their waist
And sat right down beside them.
I calmed them down.
Poor empty pants
With nobody inside them.

And, now, we meet quite often,
Those empty pants and I,
And we never shake or tremble.
We both smile
And we say
"Hi!"